# The Pariahs

# The Pariahs

*Erik Hofstatter*

Published 2014 by Creativia
Paperback design by Creativia (www.creativia.org)
ISBN: 978-9527114292
Cover art by www.busybeebookcovers.com

# Acknowledgements

I would like to mention a few special individuals who made this novella possible.
My eternal gratitude goes to: Rena Mason for her expertise and invaluable advice,
Mary SanGiovanni, Lisa Knight, Miika Hannila & Creativia Publishing.

Also, I would like to thank my loyal readers. Without you I'm nothing.


For my parents. Always.

# Contents

*Erik Hofstatter*

# PART 1: DEMYAN

# The Lockdown

 WAS asleep when they came. Two of them armed with Kalashnikovs, dressed in radiation suits. One grabbed my hair and dragged me out of the warm bed, the last time I would ever sleep on a soft mattress. The other man aimed a rifle at my face before turning it around and knocking me out with the butt.

I woke trembling on cold cement. With blurred vision I still managed to make out a shape in the distant corner—the shadow of a human body—small, immobile and frigid. I attempted to stand, but my weak legs buckled, and I collapsed back onto the filthy concrete.

Out of breath, I lay there and examined the surroundings. Stark, grey walls with cracks varying in size from hairline fractures to open fissures surrounded me like a map of veins.

The air dank and musty. The only source of light came from a tiny window covered with bars at least twenty feet above and out of reach. Two beds made of straw lined opposite walls. It appeared to be some sort of cell.

I rubbed my sore feet and noticed a small hole in the middle of the floor. No obvious toilet stood out so I came to the conclusion that this was meant to be my latrine. The body in the corner suddenly shifted. I flinched and crawled away until I backed into a wall. Long, black hair covered the face.

"Urgh...Demyan?"

The voice I recognized immediately and quickly shimmied towards it. I gently moved and held her delicate body in my arms, brushing hair from her face.

"Akilina, you're alive," I whispered tenderly.

I stared at her face for a long time. Akilina's eye was still closed; the other eye... missing. A giant lump decorated her abnormal forehead that stuck out like a Rhino's horn. Tears of joy flowed down my face. I was grateful to share the cell with my sister.

Akilina lay listless in my arms. Gathering all my strength, I rose, and walked as if carrying an anvil through quicksand, to place her frail body onto one of the straw beds. My legs and arms quivered with exhaustion for several minutes afterward.

Whilst she slept, I inspected the walls. I searched for any messages that the previous occupant might have left but found nothing. The cell's door did not budge when I pushed against them with all my might.

I considered the gutter for a moment but it was too narrow for either of us. We were trapped.

# Voice From the Deep

HE next morning, I found two bowls of porridge and couple glasses of water on the ground. How strange, I had not heard anyone come in. The shock of abduction must have taken a toll on my system. Ravenous, I ate like a beast and slowly spoon-fed Akilina. She was still weak and traumatized. Blobs of sweat formed on her giant forehead, a clear sign of fever. Stroking her black curls, I left her to sleep in peace and started to pace the dark cell, hoping an escape plan would form in my mind.

I was born with a hip deformity that made running impossible. The disaster itself had occurred more than seventeen years ago. Mother often spoke about it and how it killed my father. She also blamed his genes for our deformities.

"I should've aborted you both," she often said to me.

But I wasn't angry with her. I would have aborted myself if I had the chance. I was always different, not because of my physical abnormalities, but I saw the world differently from everyone else I knew.

I felt grotesque but at least I was blessed with intelligence. I possessed more brainpower than the other kids born after the radiation.

Mother used to scare us with stories of the government that collected naughty children and locked them away in an asylum hidden deep in the most isolated parts of Siberia, so we were always well-behaved.

I paced the cell for several minutes. How could we possibly escape? I did not even know where we were! I had no relatives except my sister and mother, both captured and locked in this hellish place.

Akilina stirred and moaned softly. I knelt beside her and felt her forehead. She was burning up fast. What could I do to decrease her temperature? Suddenly, I heard a metallic clunk, a turning of a key. Two men in suits came in, just as on the night of our abduction. I hugged my sister protectively but one of the men kicked ruthlessly and sent me flying across the cell.

The other man swung her over his shoulder like a piece of meat.

"Get off her!" I said, but my assailant pointed his gun at me. I clenched my jaw, resisting the urge to fight him.

"Leave her be! She's ill!" I pleaded in despair.

They turned around and started walking out of the cell with Akilina.

"Where are you taking her? Answer me!" I launched after him, only to be dealt a blow to my stomach.

I was a cripple, too weak to overpower them. They shut the door and left me in the cell alone. She was gone. Who knew what they would do to her? My only motivation for escape had been taken away from me and I knew I would not see her again.

Few more nights had passed in solitude. They fed me although I hardly ate; I had no reason or hope to be alive for long. Soon, my turn would come.

I crawled towards the drain to relieve myself. Then I heard it when I squatted — a feeble whisper came from the depths of the gutter.

I resisted the faecal urge and pressed my ear towards the stinking hole in the ground. A sudden smell of shit assaulted my nostrils and I felt bilious.

"Is anyone there?" I whispered into the opening, too frightened of what or who might be down there. What if it was another trap?

I was met with silence. I tried again.

"Hello? Is anyone down there?" My heart rate increased when I heard a soft answer.

"Do not be afraid. Your sister still lives..." said the voice from the deep.

# The Disaster

 FELT a sudden wave of happiness wash over me at the prospect of Akilina's survival, although her fate remained uncertain. I did not know who the voice belonged to but it was soothing and melodic and undeniably female. I pressed my ear harder against the gutter.

"How do you know that? Who are you?" I whispered down the putrid hole.

A short silence followed and I began to despair that it was all a delusion.

"She is alive...because I've seen her," the voice replied.

"Who are you? Please tell me! Are you a prisoner, too?" I pleaded.

"In a way...yes."

I bit my lip in desperation to find out more about the mysterious prisoner and what she knew of Akilina's whereabouts.

"What's your name? Do you know where we are or why we're here?"

"We are here because we're the outcasts," she said, her voice slightly louder and more coherent now. "They decided we are not worthy to coexist with *normal* people. In their eyes, we're less than human and therefore, we became *personae non gratae*—people deemed unacceptable by the government."

Perplexed by her revelation, I wondered...The outcasts? What did she mean by that? Who had the right to decide who was and wasn't normal? I leaned over the gutter once more.

"Our abduction is somehow connected to the disaster, isn't it? Because we were born after the radiation?"

"Yes, the explosion and spread of radiation was disastrous and too large to conceal by the government. Half of the world was affected but none more than us who lived closest to the nuclear reactor. You and your sister were born with deformities, correct? You and thousands of others. So many died and no one will miss us. That's why we were abducted and transported here to this...Siberian hell."

Shock and despair flowed through my veins. Mother hadn't been joking. The stories were true. The government started abducting affected children and families after the explosion. But why? Seventeen years had passed since the disaster, so why did they take us now?

I was about to voice my next question down the gutter when she voiced in alarm. "Be quiet! They're coming…"

# Gaisiya

HREE days and nights passed and still, I did not hear from her. I began to fear the worst. I remained in the dark about where we were or the purpose behind our capture. I spent days pacing the cell, trying to form some logical plan for escape, but always ended up collapsing on the bed, frustrated and exhausted. This place was like a fortress and there was no way I could break out... unless I had help.

Temporarily abandoning my hopes to see the sun ever again, I decided to accept my current predicament. To remain sane, I had to establish some kind of routine. That was going to be challenging. I could not occupy myself with books or newspapers as my captors did not provide such luxuries. They fed me and that was as far as their generosity extended.

I developed a small series of exercises and started strengthening my body every morning after breakfast. Afternoons were spent in meditation, a feeble attempt at calming my mind and increasing focus. At night, I often sat underneath the inaccessible window and pondered if I would ever hear again from my fellow prisoner down the drain.

Soon, tiredness crept over me and I lay down on the bed. I gazed at the stained ceiling and wondered what my fate would be. Was I going to die? Would I ever see Akilina and Mother again? Fear and loneliness overpowered me and I began to cry hysterically. I was all alone, and the fact of not knowing what the next day might bring absolutely terrified me. I discovered the fear of the unknown had to be the worst kind of fear a human being could possibly experience.

I had been imprisoned in this cell for eight days now. For each day that passed, I placed a single straw from Akilina's empty bed on her pillow. How long was my sentence going to be?

A month? A year? Ten years? Would this cell eventually become my tomb? But then, as I began to slowly fall into the darkest depths of despair, I heard her voice again.

"Psst! Demyan! Are you there?"

I jumped out of the bed and rushed towards the gutter. My heart pounded in my chest and I was suddenly revitalised by the prospect of hearing her sweet voice.

"Yes! I'm here! Are you okay? Did they hurt you?" I whispered into the hole.

"No, I'm okay. I wanted to talk sooner but they were watching me. I had to be careful. Did they come for you yet? Did they put you in those chains?"

"What do you mean? I've been in this cell for over a week. They bring me food but nothing more. How long have you been in this place and what is your name?"

Only silence echoed through the dark opening as I stared at it intensely. After a moment, she spoke again.

"My name is Taisiya... and I was born here."

# Conversations of the Damned

 WAS stunned. I couldn't imagine anyone being born in this cursed hellhole. How unfortunate—but if she was born here then she should know a lot more about this stronghold than I did. Surely she held some knowledge of our actual location and the purpose of this facility… and how did she know my name?

"How did you know my name?"

Taisiya spoke softly from the darkness below. "Your sister told me."

"You saw Akilina? Where is she? What have they done with her?" I roared in desperation at the mention of my sister's name.

"She's been transferred to the other block. They're preparing her for the next stage…" Taisiya's voice broke off.

"Next stage of what? What is this place? Answer me!"

"Calm down! They will hear us and they'll take you away to another cell. I'm so happy to have someone to talk to at last after all these years; I don't want to lose you."

I guess she was right. The isolation and solitude was unbearable after a week, not to mention years. Admittedly, I didn't want to lose her either. I was determined to find out more about her. I could use someone of her experience if I was ever going to flee from this place.

"I'm sorry. I'm just scared and I miss Akilina. How did you know she was my sister? When did you speak to her? Can you move freely around this prison?"

"I have ways of moving around at night," Taisiya whispered quietly, "and I came across your sister by accident. That was two nights ago. She doesn't have much time left."

My heart sank. "What do you mean? What will happen to her?"

"She—" then silence.

"Taisiya? Are you there?"

Nothing.

# Plan Imperfect

NOTHER sleepless night. I got up from the bed and paced the cell, which helped me think. I thought about Akilina and how I could possibly save her. Taisiya invaded my mind too. Her voice sounded so angelic. I wondered what her face looked like. Was she beautiful or deformed, too? It was probably the latter; otherwise, she would not be in this place. I gathered only people connected to the incident were collected by the government... and they were all sick or deformed.

There was so much I wanted to know about her. Who were her parents if she was born here? How come she was still alive after all these years yet Akilina's time was running out after only a couple of days?

I had to do something. I wondered if I could somehow break out for the night and seek her out. With her help, we could find my sister. Taisiya said she had ways of moving around the prison, but how?

Although I kept thinking about it, I never changed my conviction. There was no way I could get away from the cell. That would be impossible. The window stood too high and decorated with iron bars, the gutter too narrow, the ground made of concrete, and the door of solid steel. With no obvious shafts or pipes in sight, the only way out would be through the door.

A reckless and stupid plan formed in my mind. I decided to play dead when they brought me my next supper. Leaning over the gutter, I made myself disgorge, smearing vomit over my face and clothes. Then, I laid in the muck and waited patiently for him to come.

Hopefully, my collapse would lure him inside the cell to inspect me and then, I would ambush the man like a predator, push him over and quickly stumble out of the cell, locking the door behind me before he could restrain or shoot me.

I lay over the gutter for what seemed like hours. Suddenly, I heard the sound of a key being inserted and turned in the lock. The moment I'd been waiting for had finally arrived. I felt my body stiffen in anticipation but there was no need for theatrics. Someone unlocked the door... but no one entered.

# Whispers in the Corridors

 GOT up from the cold ground and wiped the vomit on my sleeve, uncertain what to do next. I couldn't just rush out the door and yell Akilina's name. Sitting on the bed, I anxiously waited for several minutes. Nothing.

I licked my blistered lips and exhaled. Knees trembling, I tip-toed towards the door. Pushing the lever down, I opened the door only a couple of centimetres, attempting to glimpse what lurked behind it. I saw nothing but darkness.

I listened intently but complete silence dominated the corridor I now stood in. A dim light shone couple of metres away. Leaning against the smooth wall, I started moving towards it.

The light illuminated another set of corridors. I had to be careful; my orientation skills were weak and I did not want to get lost. It was crucial for me to be able to find my way back into the cell. Most likely, I would only get one attempt at escaping this hellhole so I had to bide my time and not do anything rash or stupid.

But, whoever unlocked my cell had done so for a reason and I was intrigued to discover what that reason was. The corridors looked alike, so finding my way back would prove difficult. I moved right, silently tip-toeing with hands behind my back and feeling the wall with my fingers. Yet, all the while, I did not encounter a single soul...

I turned left into another corridor. Suspicion began to rise in me. Why wasn't anyone patrolling these corridors? Either they were so confident in the security of their impenetrable cells and building, or someone left them deliberately unprotected...

I finally noticed a set of bright double doors in the distance, and approached them with caution. Peeking through the glass, I was blinded by the white light for a split second. Then, I had to stop myself from screaming.

Akilina lay stretched across a gigantic metal bench, her arms pulled aside by long chains hanging from the ceiling. Two men in radiation suits leaned over her—one examined her face whilst the other injected something into her armpit.

Losing control, I punched the door in frustration. A sharp pain spread through my wrist and for a moment, I thought I'd broken it. When I looked up, both men were coming towards the door... towards me.

I whipped around and limped back through the corridor. I turned right on the first one and paced all the way back until I reached another set. Then, the inevitable happened. I forgot where to go next.

Adrenaline and panic rushed through my veins as I heard their footsteps behind me. I stood in the middle, looking left and right. They were so close. This was the end. I was going to die here.

"This way!" a voice whispered urgently.

It came from the left. I obeyed without hesitation—limping through the darkness until I spotted the half opened door of my cell.

"Get in quick!" another whisper echoed though the corridor.

Her voice seemed so close. I paused briefly outside my cell, frantically looking in all directions.

"Where are you? Please, let me see your face..."

Suddenly, Taisiya's voice came from behind me.

"There's no time!" she whispered harshly.

Then I was shoved through the door without getting a single glimpse at her face.

I landed on my hands and heard the lock click behind me. Turning around on my back, I lay on the ground for several minutes. Then, a wave of laughter bubbled in my gut. It felt good to be back in the sanctuary of my cell—something I never thought I would say.

# Conversations of the Damned
## Part 2

TREMBLED with fear the next morning, petrified they would figure out it was me, but they didn't. Or so it seemed. I ate my breakfast of bread and butter served with a glass of milk, pondering over the events of the previous night while I chewed the food.

It was clear Taisiya wanted me to see my sister, and she'd been the one who opened my cell and guided me through the dark corridors. I took another bite of hard bread.

The whole situation seemed risky and idiotic in retrospect. I'd ventured out of the cell with no sense of direction and with so many doors and corridors, it had been sheer luck that I found Akilina. The memory of seeing her frail body stretched across the bench in that medical room, injected with God-knows-what and not being able to help her, tormented me beyond words. Not to mention the fact I had been nearly caught.

At least now I was somewhat familiar with my surroundings outside the cell. The question was, what would I do next?

Enlisting Taisiya's help in a proper escape attempt seemed an alluring prospect. She obviously knew the area very well, being able to travel undetected and knowing how to open the cells. Her knowledge had been probably acquired through years of experience living in this stronghold. She was born here after all...

I took a gulp of sour-tasting milk.

Even if I could convince her to aid in my escape, though, I would never leave without Akilina...and Mother. I hadn't thought about her—Mother—since our abduction. My sister occupied my mind mostly, but my gut told me Mother was locked up in here too somewhere.

I decided to quiz Taisiya more in our next conversation.

Another week passed since my exploration in the corridors and still, I received no word from her. I was getting impatient and frustrated. A week in this cell felt like a year. I paced back and forth, feeling anger rising in me and ready to fall like an avalanche. What if it became her turn to be bound in those chains and she was dead? My only source of contact... my only friend in this nightmare... gone.

Was that all she meant to me? A mere friend? I searched my feelings and wondered if I felt something more for Taisiya.

The abduction, separation and isolation left me craving love and comfort. I yearned to be held by someone... someone who would assure me everything was going to be alright.

And yet, I felt something more for her. Her sweet and innocent voice, our common predicament, and bonding conversations warmed my heart. We had a connection. I smiled to myself as I began to imagine what she looked like. I had to be realistic. She was probably as deformed as the rest of us, perhaps even more...

What if she was absolutely hideous? A grotesque monster? Would it matter to me? No. Even if her face was unattractive, I would be content with the fact her personality shone with stark beauty. Her heart seemed to be in the right place—that's what mattered.

My fantasies were suddenly interrupted by light knocks coming from the depths of the gutter. I approached with caution. So far, we'd only conversed at night... never in the morning. I leaned over it and whispered gently: "Hello?"

"How was your breakfast?" Taisiya asked from below, her question accompanied by a sweet giggle.

My heart melted when I heard her voice again.

"Taisiya! It's so good to hear your voice! Where have you been? Was it you who unlocked my cell? Where did you get the key?"

"I told you I had my ways," she answered mysteriously. "I wanted you to see your sister, although not in that state..."

"But how did you know I was going to find the right room? This place is so big with so many corridors—what if I took a wrong turn and ended up somewhere completely off the grid?"

Taisiya giggled again. "I was following you, silly. If you'd taken a wrong turn, I would've told you... like I did on your way back when you got lost. Not much of a navigator, are you?"

I was slightly hurt by her confession. If she had been following me right from the start, then why didn't she reveal herself to me? I felt petrified, roaming through the corridors in the dark and not knowing where I was going or who I would encounter.

How could she let me experience that alone? I would have felt a lot safer if she'd been by my side.

"You okay? I hope I didn't upset you... I guess I was a bit insensitive. You must've been really scared and you don't know these corridors as well as I do. I'm sorry," she said sincerely.

"I'm just disappointed that you didn't show yourself to me when I asked you to."

"There was no time, Demyan. They were right behind us, you knew that."

"Why didn't you show yourself at the beginning? When you released me from my cell? I wanted to see you so badly." I countered.

Her voice trembled when she began to explain. "I couldn't...I wanted to make you happy by leading you to Akilina, give you the peace of mind that she still lived, and I watched over you in the corridors. I wouldn't let them hurt you but my face...couldn't let you see my face. I don't look normal."

"That doesn't bother me at all. I assumed you might be disfigured in some way; we all are, otherwise we wouldn't be here. I don't look normal either. I have a hip deformity."

"That affects your mobility, not the way you look," Taisiya said with a trace of melancholy in her voice. "Do you know how important it is for a girl to feel beautiful? To feel desired? No matter how hard I tried, I knew I would never feel like that. For once in my life, I felt like I had a connection with a boy, and I didn't want to ruin it by scaring you away with my face."

I paused, pondering over her confession. "Taisiya, looks aren't everything. I understand it's important for a girl to feel attractive, but what makes me sad is that most girls are so obsessed with how they look, it becomes the sole purpose of their existence. Charisma and personality are more important to me.

"Do you think people can fall in love without ever laying eyes on one another?" Taisiya asked dreamily.

"It seems absurd to most people but yes, I believe it is possible. When two strangers meet for the first time, they visually inspect each other, pondering whether they find the other person physically attractive or not. If they don't, then that's it. Suddenly they don't care about their personality or whether the person has a good heart or not. It's all about animal attraction, but if two strangers converse without ever seeing each other face to face and are given the opportunity to get to know one another, they might discover they do have a genuine connection. That connection might develop into a bond and that's how they fall in love."

"Yes, I guess you're right. So do you think we have a genuine connection?" Taisiya asked.

I felt my face turn red and was glad she could not see me. "I think we do, I like you very much," I confessed, embarrassed to admit my feelings. I hoped Taisiya wasn't secretly laughing below. To try and salvage some of my pride, I decided to change the subject quickly before she could ask any more vulnerable questions.

"So what about your parents? Are they here? How old are you?"

Taisiya didn't answer immediately. The silence stretched as if she was choosing her next words carefully. "I'm slightly older than you," she finally said. "My mother died here, giving birth to me. I never met my father."

"And you lived your entire life in the cell?" I asked, horrified by her words.

"Unfortunately, yes."

Taisiya fell silent once more but I was eager to keep the conversation flowing. She'd finally started opening up to me.

"That must've been horrible. How come you're still alive after all these years though? What is your role in all of this? You seem to know this prison very well. Why didn't you escape already?"

I never received answers to my questions.

.

# The Trial

 HEARD the lock turn once again and briefly hoped it would be Taisiya. I prayed for a chance to gaze upon her face and tell her how I really felt about her. My fantasies were shattered when the door opened and two men in radiation suits entered.

"Get up!" one of them commanded.

I obeyed without hesitation. After blindfolding me, they dragged me out of the cell. My heart pounded as we walked through the corridors towards my uncertain fate. Was this it? Was I going to die now?

The prospect of death didn't petrify me but the thought of never seeing Taisiya again did. I tried to visualize the path before me. I knew the first set of corridors but soon lost track of our direction. Perhaps they were leading me to the same room I'd seen Akilina in. And maybe she was still there. That thought calmed me down.

We stopped for a moment. One of the men let go of my arm, and I heard the unlocking of another door. The other man shoved me through and a strong scent of bleach assaulted my nostrils. I covered my nose.

"Take off your shirt," one of them said. I did, half tempted to take off my blindfold as well. He sensed my intentions and quickly added, "And if you remove the blindfold, I'll shoot you where you stand."

They forced me to lie down on a cold metal surface. I heard the rustling of chains and soon they were wrapped around my wrists. When my arms were yanked apart, I cried out in pain.

I lay there, shivering with fear for what seemed like hours. Suddenly, out of nowhere, I felt the cold needle penetrate the skin in my left armpit. I screamed when warm liquid was injected in me. My survival instinct kicked in and I started fighting against the chains but soon, my mind slipped into oblivion.

# The Reflection

WOKE up on the straw bed in the sanctuary of my cell, without a clue how long I'd been out. My armpit was red and itchy but apart from that, I didn't feel any different. What was that liquid they injected me with?

I rose from the bed and the entire cell started spinning. I lay back down and closed my eyes, exhausted from the trauma. What the hell was going to happen to me? I began reflecting on my life, trying to figure out where I'd gone wrong to deserve such a cruel fate.

My childhood was bit of a blur. Father died during the explosion and Mother worked endless hours to support me and my sister. Instead of playing with the other kids, I cleaned the flat while Mother rested after work. I disliked collecting Akilina from school as it was such a long way away and walking was painful for me because of my hip.

I was a bit of a rebel at school and my teachers hated me. Not because I was stupid, but I was a bad influence. I enjoyed entertaining other pupils and being the centre of attention. Ultimately, I was expelled from school because I accepted a risky dare from one of my so-called friends.

We were in the classroom, waiting for our next lesson to begin, and he dared me to climb out of the window and walk along the sill. It was a four storey building and we were on the third floor. Back then, in the middle of November, in the freezing cold, there was no doubt I would die if I slipped. Still, I wanted to prove to him I could do it, that I wasn't afraid. The next day I was called into the principal's office with my friend standing there.

He described the whole story, how I'd climbed out of the window like a madman, ironically leaving out the part about how it had all been his idea, and I was expelled. That was the first day I learned about betrayal.

# Conversations of the Damned
# Part 3

 CRAWLED towards the hole when I heard the distant knocking. The prospect of speaking to Taisiya seemed attractive after my horrifying ordeal. If only she could hold me.

"Hey, are you there?" I whispered down the drain, my voice slightly trembling.

"Yeah, I'm here. Are you alright? Is it true they took you?"

"It's true," I said painfully. "They came last night. What have they done to me, Taisiya?"

She went quiet for a few minutes. "Have you noticed any changes in your body? Do you feel any different?" she asked.

"No…not yet," I answered. "Why? What kind of changes?"

"Look at the colour of your fingers. Do they seem darker? Black, even?"

My hands trembled as I inspected the colour of my fingers. They looked normal.

"I don't see any changes, but the cell is very dim."

"Oh, good! Sounds like you were given the placebo." Taisiya breathed out a sign of relief.

"What do you mean? And what about Akilina?"

"I don't know about your sister, but I discovered which cell she is in. If I let you out again, you might be able to talk to her."

Suddenly, I felt my head clear as my alertness increased. The memory of Akilina stretched on the table in that horrifying room invaded my mind, and I knew I had to see her, make sure she was alright.

"So you could let me out again? But how would I find her? I don't know where her cell is."

25

"I will leave clues for you in the corridors. Look for shards of broken glass. If you reach a point where you don't know where to go next, look around. If you see any pieces of glass, that's the direction you should go in. Her cell is not far from yours anyway, and I will place a shard in front of her door, too."

Adrenaline coursed through my veins. "We could just go together," I suggested.

"I can't. Get some rest and tomorrow night, I will open your door after dinner. I'll make sure the corridors are empty, too. Good luck, Demyan."

# Whispers in the Corridors Part 2

 HE following night, I was ready. I ate my meal in haste and anxiously anticipated the moment of my temporary release. Seeing Akilina was all I cared about—that was the sole purpose of my mission. I simply had to put my sister first.

I felt the invisible knot tightening my insides when the door unlocked. As before, I waited several minutes to make sure no one would come in. Then, I crept out of the cell.

Once more, the corridors appeared deserted. I stayed close to the wall, moving silently through the passages. When I reached the first intersection, I saw a smashed bulb near one of the lights, and moved towards it.

That particular passage seemed like an endless tunnel. Keeping my pace slow, it felt like I walked for hours. Then, I saw a figure in the distance, standing directly below the next light. I froze, unsure how to react. The shape looked in my direction and, with one lightning motion, smashed the bulb. The broken shards fell on the ground. I licked my lips and stepped into the darkness.

This area was unfamiliar to me. It looked different from the last corridor and I sensed I was getting closer to my destination. As I turned left on the next intersection, I spotted a row of illuminated cell doors. The light above the last cell was broken. *Akilina must be here...*

I couldn't stand the thought of my little sister being trapped inside that horrible cell, and I nearly attempted to sprint towards the last door. But I didn't, for I was distracted by distant voices. They were moving towards me so I retreated, slowly sinking into the dark, but making sure I remained within hearing distance.

"Her response to the treatment is rather fascinating," said a male voice, "and a significant progress has been made but as you know, her chances for a complete transformation are miniscule."

I leaned closer to the wall, too scared to breathe. Was he referring to Akilina?

"Good news indeed, Doctor. I'm pleased my daughter is getting better, slowly but surely. I would be grateful if you could keep me updated on any changes… big or small," a female voice answered.

Something about that voice sounded very familiar. Then the realization slapped me in the face.

*Mother.*

# Forget Me

COVERED my mouth with both hands, trying to control the hyper-ventilation. Had it really been her or was I hallucinating? I could not see the woman's face but the voice was undeniably Mother's. I had a sudden urge to confront her but decided to remain hidden. The risk would be too great if I was mistaken.

I must have been mistaken. Mother wouldn't let us rot in this filth, being experimented on or whatever they were doing to us. I waited patiently for them to leave and then I moved through the shadows closer to the cell.

I lay my hands on the door and softly whispered Akilina's name. No answer. I tried again. "Akilina! Are you there?"

Then, someone slipped a folded piece of paper underneath the door. I looked left and right, making sure I was still alone.

My fingers trembled as I unfolded the paper. I could not read the note in the surrounding darkness so I folded it again and placed it in my pocket.

"Akilina, is that you?" I said urgently through the door. I waited for a few seconds. Then I knocked but no one answered.

"Akilina, please! Say something if you're in there! It's Demyan!"

I was distracted by a debilitating noise that sounded like some kind of a siren. I couldn't afford to waste any more time. In a panic, I limped back through the corridors, yearning for the safety of my own cell. This time, I remembered the way back. It only took me several minutes.

I shut the door behind me and collapsed on my bed, panting. The siren eventually ceased and I closed my eyes, unable to believe my luck. I'd made it back for the second time.

I lay there for a while, processing all I had seen and heard. Then I remembered the mysterious note. I pulled it out of my pocket and unfolded it. Only a few words

29

were written on the paper, words that made me cry as I read them: FORGET ME AND SAVE YOURSELF. AKILINA.

The words were written in blood.

# The Panic

READ her message over and over again, the words *'save yourself'* echoing in my head. I started to pace the length of the cell, hoping it would calm me. But to no avail. The more desperate I got, the more I felt the panic setting in. What was I going to do next? *Forget the message, that's what.*

I wouldn't leave this place without my sister. Different escape scenarios swam in my mind but none were realistic. Finally, anger pushed me over the edge. I started kicking and punching the cell's door, yelling, "LET ME OUT! I WANT TO SEE MY SISTER! DO YOU HEAR ME? OPEN THIS DOOR RIGHT NOW!"

I kept up the racket for several minutes, hoping someone would eventually hear me. I didn't know what to expect. Of course, they wouldn't let me see Akilina just like that but I was curious to find out what they would do if I behaved aggressively.

The lock turned and I realized I was going to find out very soon. An armed man in a radiation suit entered my cell. I didn't know if it was a different man or the same one as before as they all looked alike.

"What do you want?" he enquired in an even tone.

"I want to see my sister and make sure she's alright," I replied, trying to sound confident.

He stood there for a few seconds as if contemplating what to do next.

"Okay," he finally said.

As he approached me, he flipped the machine gun and drove the butt in my face with full force. And then, I saw no more.

# The Experiment Room

AWOKE on the cold bench again, temporarily blinded by the bright light. Aching to shield my eyes, I couldn't for my arms were stretched apart by heavy chains. My mouth felt dry and I tried to generate some saliva. Then, a blurry face leaned over mine.

"Hello, Demyan. How are you feeling?"

My vision cleared after couple of seconds and I looked at the face. I did not recognize it.

"That was some blow you took, my friend," the voice said, with what sounded like genuine concern.

There was something vaguely familiar in that concerned and reassuring tone. I'd heard it before. Giving the man a sharp glance, I realized this was the same doctor I'd heard outside Akilina's cell with the woman whose voice strangely resembled my mother's. He seemed to be in charge or definitely high up enough to provide some answers.

"Who are you? Where am I?" I began, still struggling in the chains.

"Relax, Demyan, don't exert your energy needlessly," the doctor answered, and placed his warm hand on my forehead. "I'm willing to answer some of your questions but only if you promise to calm down," he added, piercing me with his hypnotic eyes.

I felt my body relax under his gaze.

"Where is my sister? What are you doing to her?" I asked in a calmer manner. I had so many questions and I was eager to get them answered.

He smiled and removed his hand. "Your sister is in a separate room, as I'm sure you know. We are in a biomedical research facility, which I believe you also know. You and your sister have been selected for our clinical trials. You should consider yourself lucky, Demyan, as you and Akilina are contributing greatly to the advancement of treating human diseases. We also study Genetics here. I'm not sure if you know what that means exactly so I will enlighten you. Genetics is the process of trait inheritance, from parents to offspring, including the molecular structure and function of genes. We have been specializing in genetic research for the last seventeen years or so, studying different families affected by the radiation."

"Aha! So the government is responsible for this!" I exclaimed.

The doctor held my gaze, his expression unreadable.

"What gives you the right to abduct us from our beds and experiment on us like we are rats? Why does the government allow this?" I continued with my protests.

He seemed puzzled. "You think the government is responsible? Oh, dear Demyan, it's not the government who put you here..."

Now it was my turn to be confused and hold his gaze.

"Who is responsible, then?"

"Well, we receive many volunteers," he said upon a sigh, "but in your case it was a parental request. Your mother is the sole reason why both of you are here."

Shell-shocked, I said no more as I calmly watched the injection sink into my armpit.

# The Request

LET them escort me back into my cell, feeling tranquilized. They pushed me over the threshold and I sat on the edge of the bed, my head bowed in despair. This was the ultimate betrayal.

For the entire period of our imprisonment, I'd held the government responsible. Never in my darkest dreams would I have suspected my own mother. The more I thought about it, the more it made sense.

Her phrase, "I should've aborted you both..." echoed in my mind over and over again. We didn't turn out the way she'd hoped. She was very disappointed about our deformities, made that clear from the start, and I guess this was her way of erasing us from her life. But why was she checking on our progress? She said she wanted to be updated on any changes, big or small.

Surely, if she wanted to erase us from her life, she would have just left us here without looking back. I was puzzled by her motive. What was I going to do now? Was I supposed to accept the fact my mother never loved us? And that we were going to spend the rest of our days as human guinea pigs?

Another week passed. The doctor's revelation broke my spirit completely, so I spent most of the time lying on the bed in total hopelessness. I still couldn't believe my very own mother had subjected us to this hell...

Why did it matter so much to her how we looked? A mother should love her children no matter what. Now we had no one... and I did not know what else to do.

Freeing Akilina seemed more impossible than ever before, even with Taisiya's help. I just had nothing else to give. Where would we go? What would we do?

We were imprisoned in the middle of Siberia, with hostile temperatures and surrounded by an ocean of snow. It was hopeless...

Yet, I couldn't accept my fate. I wouldn't let them inject us with unknown chemicals until we died. We were both so young, with our whole lives before us. I had to escape... or die trying. I somehow believed that our destiny lay outside of these walls, that we were both fated for greater things. Something brewed inside me that they couldn't get to—hope.

Determination coursed through my veins and again, I started to weigh several escape scenarios. The plan had to involve Taisiya. She was the only one who knew this stronghold inside out and she could move around the site undetected; she had access to cell keys and various other valuable items.

I had to convince her to help us. First, she would carry a message to Akilina, letting her know when to be ready.

She would then prepare warm clothing for us, as well as food, maps, etc. On the night of the escape, she would unlock my sister's cell and bring her to me...then she would lead us out.

It sounded simple but I was sure the reality would be quite different. I wondered if she would come with us...but then again she'd had many opportunities for escaping in the past yet she chose to stay. Why? What was her true connection to this place?

I hadn't spoken to her in over a week. Where was she? I hoped nothing had happened to her; she was the key to our freedom.

The following night I attempted to make contact with her. I leaned over the gutter and softly called out her name.

"Are you down there, Taisiya? I need to speak with you! Hello?"

She answered after several seconds.

"I'm here, Demyan. Are you alright? I've heard they injected you again..."

I had almost forgotten about the trial. I didn't feel any different so I assumed it was just another placebo.

"Yes, I feel fine. It was just another placebo..."

"Are you sure, Demyan? Sometimes it takes a while for the drug to start working..."

I didn't consider that. "Well, a whole week has passed so I'm sure it's fine. If they gave me the real thing surely it would take effect after couple of hours, right?"

"Not necessarily...but let's not worry about that now," she said with a hint of cheeriness.

I imitated her positive tone in my next question.

"Taisiya...I need your help. Would you be able to get us outta here?"

She did not speak for some time so I decided to carry on convincing her.

"I know it would be extremely dangerous for all of us but we can't stay here. One of these days they will inject us with the real drug and then we're dead. There's so much more to life, Taisiya. You must help us!" I pleaded.

"But...where would you go? You would freeze to death outside..." she finally said, confused and petrified.

"I would rather take our chances of surviving in the Siberian wilderness than stay here and slowly await our death, which would be quite gruesome I'm sure. You know this place better than anyone and you have access to keys. Would you be able to get some food and warm clothes for us? Perhaps even a map of the area?" I asked hopefully.

"I think so," Taisiya said uncertainly.

"Good! Then we can start planning straight away! Let me know how soon you can put these items together and then you will need to inform Akilina. Once she is aware of our plans, you will get her out and take her here. We can then follow your lead outside."

"There's a small problem…" she said.

"What is it? I'm sure we can think of an alternative solution," I replied, full of determination. It felt good to finally have a purpose.

"They moved Akilina to a different cell and I don't know where. We're also running out of time. There are things you don't know about, Demyan. I will try to get you out as I greatly care about you, but only you. I don't have enough time to search for your sister and getting both of you out would be too dangerous. Also, I can't come with you. You would be all alone in the middle of Siberia. Are you sure this is what you want?"

Now it was my turn to be silent. Taisiya's words hit me hard. Escaping without Akilina was something I did not consider before. After our mother's betrayal, she was the only family I had left. I couldn't abandon her.

"I can't leave without my sister," I said tearfully, "and why can't you come? Do you enjoy being trapped in this nightmare? Is it because you were born here and this prison is all you've ever known?"

"I would love to come with you but it's simply impossible. I can't leave. Please, Demyan, if you want to escape now is the time. I would continue my search for Akilina once you're gone and perhaps I would be able to get her out later…"

It wasn't exactly a foolproof plan but I had no choice. "Alright, prepare some clothes and food for me. Try to find a map of the local area. There must be a shack or somewhere I can hide for a while. Once I'm safely out, I will think of what to do next. How long will you need?"

"I should be able to collect the supplies by tomorrow night. I will unlock your cell after dinner and leave a rucksack next to the door. I will also include a hand drawn map of the corridors that will guide you to the nearest fire exit. You're lucky as your cell is very close to it and once more I will arrange for the corridors to be empty so you will be able to find the door undisturbed."

"I don't know how to thank you, Taisiya," I said truthfully." I only wish you and Akilina could come with me."

"Perhaps we will meet one day...in more pleasant surroundings." She laughed ever so sweetly.

"One day..." I whispered.

# Unmasked

 WAS ready the following night, both mentally and physically. The prospect of freedom energized me more than the meagre supper of borscht I had just eaten. My knees trembled as I paced the cell, anxiously waiting for Taisiya to open the door.

I hoped with all my heart that everything would go according to plan. Leaving Akilina behind gnawed on me more than I wanted to admit but I had to believe Taisiya would free her too, even if little bit later.

A click of the lock interrupted my thoughts. I waited for a few minutes as before, just to make sure it was Taisiya and not one of the guards. No one came in so I opened the door slowly. Poking my head out, I looked in both directions. The corridors were deserted.

I tip-toed out of the cell and closed the door behind me, taking care not to make a sound. I was relieved to discover an overstuffed rucksack next to the cell. It was dark and I had no time to check the contents—I trusted Taisiya.

Underneath the rucksack sat a folded piece of paper, I assumed this was the map that would guide me to the fire exit. I swung the rucksack over my shoulder, slightly surprised that it wasn't as heavy as it looked.

I limped to the nearest lamp and unfolded the paper. The drawing was very primitive and childlike, as if drawn in a hurry. It showed a big "X" not far from where I stood so I started walking towards my freedom, slowly at first and then picking up my pace.

I tried to be cautious as I hurried through the corridors, but my excitement proved hard to control. Following the map turned out to be an easy task and I was nearly there.

I took a final turn and spotted a set of green doors in the distance. The bar was wrapped in a chain and my heart sank for a second before I realized someone had dropped the lock and the chain hung loose. This was it. The outside world stretched a couple of steps away...

My hands shook as I pressed the bar and pushed the door open. The gust of freezing wind hit me in the face.

*I did it! I'm finally free!*

Dropping the rucksack, I pulled out something furry from the side pocket, pleased to discover an ushanka and a pair of gloves. Feeling grateful, I put on the warm hat and then, something strange happened when I was putting on the gloves.

The fingers in my left hand began to tingle. At first, I thought it could be the cold but the feeling was too intense and started spreading through my arm. In a panic, I removed the glove and found myself horrified to see the tips of my fingers turning black!

What was happening to me? I started hyperventilating and it became increasingly difficult to breathe. Something was wrong...

A sharp pain in my chest made me collapse and I felt myself slipping into unconsciousness. Just then, a figure dressed in white leaned over me. Was I dead? The person gave me a violent shake.

"Demyan! Wake up! Do you hear me? Demyan!"

I tried to focus on the face above my own. My eyes cleared for a few seconds, long enough for me to see the wrinkly face of an old woman. What had seemed like a white dress before now appeared light blue... I recognized the uniform—a nurse's apron. The old woman even had on a nurse's hat...

"Please, help me! I'm dying!" I mumbled.

"Stay with me, Demyan! I won't let you die after everything we've been through!" she cried.

"What do you mean? Who are you?" I asked at the brink of death.

"I'm Taisiya..." whispered the nurse.

# PART 2: AKILINA

# Kidnapped

I CRIED, watching them drag my brother out of his bed. One of the men beckoned to me but I did not hear him as every sound in our room was drowned by my own screams when the other man struck Demyan with his rifle.

I was so terrified, I didn't want them to hurt me, too. The man pulled me out of my bed and blindfolded me. The last thing I saw was my brother being dragged away, unconscious.

A sudden wave of panic took hold of me and I started screaming mommy's name. I wanted her to help us, to save us from these intruders. Snatching away my blindfold, I ran into the kitchen, desperately searching for my mommy, but it was empty. Then I ran into the living room, screaming and crying at the same time. She wasn't there, either.

I headed for the bedroom but was yanked back by my hair with brutal force. Something wet and cold was shoved on my face. I felt sleepy, then, within moments, I saw and felt nothing more.

A while later, I opened my eyes and moaned softly as something prickly stuck into my back. I felt feverish and sick all over. I called my brother's name.

"Urgh...Demyan?"

As if by some miracle, I dreamed I saw his face before mè. He caressed me and gently brushed my hair out of my face. He seemed so happy to hold me in his arms. Then the dream ended and I saw nothing but darkness.

# The Separation

'M not sure for how long I slept. When I woke up, Demyan's face was leaning over mine. This time I knew he was real; it wasn't a hallucination. I felt so weak, I hardly had the strength to open my mouth and swallow whatever he was feeding me but I also felt overwhelmed with happiness and security that my big brother was beside me, for he would look after us.

The food did not energize me. Blobs of sweat formed on my forehead. In the corner of my eye, I saw Demyan pacing the cell impatiently, trying to think of a way to free us, no doubt. I felt sleepy again and started to drift off when I heard the door open.

My brother launched himself over me in a protective gesture. I was so hot and sweaty, I couldn't keep up with everything that was happening around me.

Next thing I noticed was my brother crouching in the corner and then, the large man swung me over his shoulder. I didn't have the strength to fight him. I heard my brother's screams of protest.

"Leave her be! She's ill!"

Then his voice ceased and I fainted.

# Mutual Friend

HE new cell looked similar to the previous one. I don't remember much after the separation. Several days passed but I couldn't tell for sure, I lost all sense of time. My brother's presence had helped me feel safe but now, all alone, I was petrified. I curled up on the bed, which was made of straw and just as uncomfortable as the last one.

Some bread and water sat on a tray in the corner but I wasn't hungry. I missed Demyan and my mommy. Who knew why they'd kidnapped us or where we were held, but I hoped Mommy would rescue us soon. She had no money but I was sure she would find some solution; I just had to be patient.

In the morning, I was visited by an elderly woman. At first I was scared of her but she was dressed like a nurse and had a very sweet and reassuring voice.

"Do not be afraid of me, child. I'm not going to hurt you," she said.

The nurse sat on the edge of the bed and patted the empty patch next to her. "Come and sit next to me, child. I want to look at you and make sure you're alright."

I hesitated but did as I was told. She had a warm smile and piercing ocean-blue eyes. I returned her smile and shivered as she felt my forehead.

"How are you feeling, dear?"

I hesitated once more but decided to communicate with the nurse. "I'm okay, still feeling hot and I really miss my brother," I confessed.

"Oh, poor child! Where is your brother?" she asked, full of concern.

"We were kidnapped and thrown into a cell together but they separated us. Please, will you help us?" I pleaded in despair.

She embraced me lovingly and stroked my hair. "I'll do my best to help you, child. What is your brother's name?"

"I'm Akilina and his name is Demyan."

"Demyan..." she whispered. "I'll try and find him—let him know you're safe. You must rest now, dear." She kissed my head and started walking out of the cell.

"What is your name?" I called after the nurse.

She briskly turned around. "Taisiya," she answered with a fading smile.

# The Hallucination

BROWSED through the colourful pictures of *Runaway Bunny* when two men in strange suits entered the cell. I nearly screamed but knew it was no use. They were gentler this time, so I wondered if it had anything to do with the nice nurse.

They ordered me to stand. I did and followed the first man out of the cell while the other walked behind me. All the secrecy and the fact of not knowing where they were taking me filled me with terror. For a brief moment, I hoped they might be taking me to see my mommy. Perhaps she paid the ransom and they were going to release us. My heart sank when we entered a huge room with a silver table in the middle.

"Take off your clothes and lie down," one of the men said.

It took me several seconds to understand him as his voice was muffled by the mask.

"No," I said, and began to sob.

He aimed the gun at me then, so I did as I was told and began to undress. The table felt so cold on my bare skin that I started to shiver. Chains hung loosely from the ceiling. The other man wrapped them around my wrists, then, he pulled my arms apart.

"Have no fear," he said whilst picking up a large injection needle.

As he approached me with it, I turned my head towards the doors. I moaned softly when the sharp needle pierced my skin. Soon, I began to hallucinate. For a brief moment, I saw my brother's face through the glass in the doors. I smiled when I saw tears in his eyes. He banged on the doors but then, I saw him no more.

# The Note

HEN I woke up, I didn't feel any different. My skin was raw and itchy and I kept scratching at it until it bled. That night I was visited by a doctor who examined my face. He smelled funny and his humming annoyed me.

"Good, good," he muttered. "You're making excellent progress."

I didn't understand what he was talking about so I just sat in silence, thinking about my brother—wondering if he was going through the same thing.

As he exited the cell, I caught a glimpse of a woman who resembled Mommy. My heart skipped a beat and I nearly cried out. Then, the door closed and I realized it had probably been one of the other nurses.

I sat on the bed and thought about Demyan. I prayed we could escape together, find Mommy and forget this horrible experience ever happened to us. My armpit was itching again so I slid my hand under my tunic and scratched it hard. It stung and I felt something cold slide against my ribs.

When I lifted the garment, I saw a stream of blood flowing from my armpit. My finger nails were so long, I had scratched the skin too hard. The blood kept coming but then I was distracted by a voice outside my cell.

"Akilina! Are you there?" the voice whispered.

I thought I was dreaming. I cried with joy when I heard my brother's voice. I knew he wouldn't have left me to rot in this filth.

Yet, as much as I longed to be in my brother's arms, I suddenly realized the cruel reality. We would never make it out alive, not together anyway. I didn't have the strength to voice my words so I picked up *Runaway Bunny* and tore out the last page that was blank.

By then, my armpit stopped bleeding so I dug my nails into it once more. Soon a trail of blood flowed from it and I had the ink I needed. I wrote the words: FORGET ME AND SAVE YOURSELF. AKILINA.

After slipping the note under the door, I collapsed on the bed. A river of tears flooded my face as I listened to Demyan's desperate pleas.

"Akilina, is that you? Akilina, please! Say something if you're in there! It's Demyan!"

It was torture. I covered my mouth with both hands just to stop my shrieks from escaping but my will wasn't strong enough. I jumped out of the bed and kneeled before the door, ready to answer my brother's calls.

"Dem—" I started to say but the deafening siren drowned my voice.

# We All Perish

**T**HEY moved me to another cell shortly after. I'm not sure why; perhaps they suspected Demyan knew where I was and this would prevent him from ever finding me again. It worked. My new cell was hidden in the deepest part of the facility.

When they transferred me, I had a good look around. They didn't blindfold me this time; I wasn't a threat anymore, I suppose, or maybe they wanted me to know I had no chance of escaping. Truth be told, escaping never crossed my mind. I was patiently waiting for Mommy to get us out.

Even nurse Taisiya, who often visited me before, stopped coming. Either I was in a restricted ward or she'd lost interest in me. Time went on; sometimes they took me away for two injections a day. In some instances, I felt really sick afterwards and stayed in bed for days. My hope was fading and I was slowly dying.

At last, the next evening, after supper, she came to see me. She seemed distressed.

"Hello, how are you feeling, dear?" she asked, unable to hide the melancholy in her voice.

I cleared my throat. "I'm okay, thank you," I answered. My voice was husky from the lack of use.

"That's good," she said, stroking my hair. Tears welled up in her eyes.

"What's the matter? Why are you sad?" I asked her as softly as I could.

She kept stroking my hair in silence, as if trying to find courage or the right words.

Eventually, she found both. "Oh, child, I don't know how to tell you this," she began. "Your brother tried to escape…"

Nurse Taisiya's revelation pleased me at first, but as I watched her teary face it became clear he didn't make it.

"He got caught, didn't he?" I asked, lowering my eyes and suppressing my own tears.

"No," she whispered, clearing her voice before continuing. "He…collapsed while escaping. They dragged him to the infirmary for examination. He was in a bad state."

I couldn't hold my tears back any longer. "Is he going to be alright?"

She reached out to me and hugged me tightly. "I'm so sorry, child," she said whilst stroking my back. "He died this morning of multiple organ failure."

Her words took a few seconds to sink in before my whole world crumbled.

Then, darkness swallowed all.

# New Light

SHE comforted me for a long time but nothing could stop the endless river of tears. I mourned for weeks, still unable to come to terms with my brother's death. I loved him so much and couldn't face another day in this world without him. I stopped eating but the men in strange suits came in and force-fed me. They were so cruel; why couldn't they just let me die peacefully?

In the early days I had hoped Mommy would get us out but after Demyan's death, I lost faith even in her. Why was it taking so long for her to find us? Surely, our kidnappers had contacted her and demanded some sort of payment. Did she refuse? I wished someone would explain to me what was going on...

I was lost—couldn't figure out whether to keep hoping Mommy would find me or whether I should just accept my fate and wait for them to kill me, too.

For some reason, they stopped injecting me for a while after nurse Taisiya's last visit. Perhaps they wanted to give me time to mourn—or planning something more sinister.

More time passed in this limbo, when I endlessly drifted between life and death. All my hope had flown out this cursed place. Nurse Taisiya came in again that night and we spoke about Demyan for a long time. It turned out she knew him more than I thought.

She told me of their bonding conversations at night and how she'd befriended him. It seemed like we talked for hours and I was shocked when she confessed that it was she who'd helped to organise his failed escape.

"Why did you want to help him?" I asked her.

"I don't know," she answered, lowering her eyes. "I have worked here for so long and witnessed so much suffering over the years. That first night, when I informed him of your survival, he was so happy! I sensed so much joy and hope in his voice, I didn't have the heart to tell him the truth about who I really was," she confessed.

I didn't know what to think. She seemed like a sincere person who was telling the truth, but she also worked for the kidnappers. Should I trust her or not?—a question I couldn't answer yet...

"I convinced myself it would comfort him more if he thought I was a prisoner too so I created an illusion," she continued with her confession.

I took her hand in mine. "You tried your best to help him," I said reassuringly. "That's what matters. His death wasn't your fault."

Towards the end of our conversation, Nurse Taisiya shocked me even more with a daring proposal.

"I want you to carry on, child," she said.

"What do you mean?" I asked, tired and confused.

"I want you to continue where your brother failed. I want you to escape," Taisiya replied, her voice full of determination.

Suddenly, I felt scared. Escaping with Demyan had seemed like a realistic idea but I could never make it by myself.

"I'm just a kid," I said to her. "Where would I go?"

"There was nothing wrong with my original plan. It was effective...it would've worked. It was just bad timing...what happened to Demyan. I will provide food, clothing, maps—and I will collect you myself this time. I will lead you to the exit. Please, child, I will never forgive myself for deceiving your brother. You must let me atone for my sins. Let me help you."

It was insane. She wanted me to follow the same plan my brother had—the same plan that led to his death, but there was also a surprise addition to her plan.

"There is an abandoned hut about two miles from here," Taisiya continued with her proposal. "It's covered in snow and will be hard to find but if you manage to find it and wait for me there, I will take you somewhere safe after I finish my shift."

I listened to her and pondered every word. In truth, I was eager to see my mommy and now that Demyan was gone, there was no reason for me to stay. I was too young to die, so I would do it for my brother—succeed where he'd failed. If he was watching me from heaven, he would have wanted me to go with nurse Taisiya.

We talked it through some more and decided that tomorrow, after dinner, I would make my escape.

#  The White Plains of Siberia

 Y last night in the cell was a sleepless one. I rolled over and over on my straw bed, unable to shut down my brain. Chaotic thoughts raced each other like a pack of greyhounds. What if I got caught? What if I couldn't find the hut and freeze to death? What if she didn't turn up? What if it was a trap?

I was petrified but at the same time, I had to try. Their injections would kill me eventually so the way I saw it, I had nothing to lose and plenty to gain.

My lack of sleep during the night took its toll, so I slept for most of the day, only getting up to collect my meagre breakfast. I wanted to be well-rested, to conserve my energy.

The rest of the day, I drifted in and out of sleep. During the waking moments, I carefully examined the plan in my mind, trying to avoid the negative thoughts of all the scenarios that could possibly go wrong. At last, the hour was almost upon me. I ate my last meal in silence and waited for Nurse Taisiya.

I didn't have to wait long; soon after dinner, she came to collect me.

"Hurry, child, we don't have much time," she urged.

I reached for my *Runaway Bunny* book, the only object in my cell that cheered me up.

"Leave that, there's no time!" Nurse Taisiya said.

I noticed a rucksack on her shoulder so I snatched the book anyway. Smiling tenderly as if regretting her curt tone, she took it from my hand and placed it in the large sack.

Nurse Taisiya locked the empty cell behind us and grabbed my hand. Her skin felt different from my mommy's—rough, rugged, and her hand very large.

"Hurry, we must run!"

The corridors stretched ahead, dark and silent. I had no idea where we were or how far we had to run. Luckily for us, it wasn't far at all. We turned left and found ourselves in front of large green doors. Nurse Taisiya pushed the bar and the freezing wind rattled my hair.

She laid down the rucksack and pulled out some clothes along with a thick, furry sweater.

"It's very cold outside. You need to wear all these layers," she said while helping me with the warm sweater.

When I was fully dressed, she shoved a piece of paper in my hand.

"This is the map of the local area," she said.

I glanced at her with a puzzled look. "I don't know how to read maps," I replied sheepishly.

She chuckled and stroked my cheek. "Don't be scared, child. I made it really easy for you. You'll be fine."

We unfolded the paper and looked at it together. Nurse Taisiya pointed at a red cross.

"This is where we are and this is where you need to go," she said while pointing at a green circle. "The journey is straightforward and shouldn't take more than an hour. When you get to the hovel, wait for me there. There is an old fireplace you can use to keep warm and I packed plenty of food for you. It will be dark soon so you must hurry!"

She wrapped the woolly scarf around my neck and shoved me out of the door.

"Hurry, child! Wait for me there and I will collect you soon," she promised.

With a final smile, she shut the door behind her and disappeared. I threw the rucksack over my shoulder and immediately staggered under its weight. Nurse Taisiya obviously overestimated my strength. This was going to be a struggle. I wasn't sure if I could make it that far in deep snow with a heavy burden on my back...but I had to.

I unfolded the map once more and looked at the markings. I felt bad for lying to her. Demyan had taught me how to read maps ages ago and I was very good at it. I studied the map for a few minutes and decided on my next destination.

I wasn't going to wait for Taisiya. I wasn't going to find the hut. I was going to find my mommy instead. With my brother gone, she was all I had left. I couldn't wait to see her. I wanted her to hug me so badly.

With the thought of Mommy's loving embrace, I turned away from the facility and marvelled at the white plains of Siberia that stretched before me.

# PART 3: TAISIYA

# Fresh Arrivals

HEY pencilled me in for a morning shift that week but I requested to work nights instead. I had been a head nurse in the institution for over twenty years, so I had the seniority to work whichever hours suited me best. Having been an owl for most of my life, I preferred the quiet of the night. It was hectic during the day when most of the trials took place and I didn't want to witness any of them.

I knew some of the conducted trials here were illegal but the job paid well so I didn't ask any questions. They always paid me cash in hand at the end of the month, and that was fine by me.

Two new arrivals were also scheduled in that week—a brother and a sister, aged seventeen and twelve. My duties as a head nurse included to check on them. I entered the nurses' station and picked up a clipboard from the metal shelf. The notes stated the siblings were kept in separate cells, so I decided to check on the girl first. Females were always easier to handle—more emotional but less impulsive. I read her file and made my way down to cell 201.

I unlocked the door and saw the girl sitting in a corner, flipping through a book. She winced when she saw me enter.

"Don't be afraid of me, child. I'm not going to hurt you," I said as sweetly as I could.

She was terrible to behold, certainly one of the more extreme cases of radiation aftermath we'd had in recent years. I sat on the edge of the bed and invited her to sit beside me.

I enquired about her health whilst examining her gigantic forehead. The conversation turned towards her brother. I'd already familiarized myself with his file too and knew he was in the cell directly above the nurses' station.

I promised to the child that I would seek her brother out and let him know she was alright. Of course, I played this charade only to gain her trust, which wasn't hard given her naiveté and young age.

After leaving her cell, I returned to the station and made myself a cup of coffee. Nights at the institution were long and boring so I decided to have some fun with my new meat.

# The Illusion

 WAS the only nurse on duty that night. Therefore, I could proceed with my entertainment undisturbed. Moving the chair from the table close to the sewage pipe that led through the wall, I proceeded with my game. The smell was appalling but all the nurses were used to it now. I stood on the chair and whispered through the small opening.

I listened carefully. He took the bait and countered with questions almost immediately.

"Do not be afraid, your sister still lives..." I whispered up to him, and took a sip of my steaming coffee.

An entertaining conversation followed. The lad was bright and I genuinely began to like him. I invented a theory for why he was here and how the government collected people affected by the radiation. He believed me so perhaps he wasn't that bright after all. Still, it was nice to have some company for a change.

We talked for the rest of my shift but soon, it was time for me to go home.

"Be quiet! They're coming..." I whispered to end our exchange.

Finishing my coffee, I collected my things, ready to leave. I locked the station and switched off the lights.

# Watcher in the Dark

 WAS off for three days and looked forward to another talk with the boy. During the time away from work, I wondered how I could amuse myself further. Then, I had a genius idea! I would unlock his cell and watch what he would do. Yes—what an entertaining notion.

I hung my coat on the hanger and looked around to make sure no one was listening.

"Psst! Demyan! Are you there?" I said into the opening.

He answered at once, sounding so relieved to hear my voice! I enjoyed the dominion I had over him, as well as the fact he regarded me as some kind of a saviour. Another conversation ensued. Shortly thereafter, I decided to leave him be, and headed down the corridor to open his cell. I was quite excited to see how he would react. It would be like watching a rat in a maze.

I turned the lock and quickly retreated into the darkness, patiently waiting for him to come out. Several minutes passed, during which the door remained closed. What was he doing in there?

Finally, he emerged. The boy moved through the darkness with extreme caution. I followed, silently observing from the shadows. I knew his sister was scheduled for a trial that night. Thus, I hoped he would follow the right path and find the experiment room.

Luckily, he did. Demyan crouched down and slowly looked through the door. Suddenly, he startled me by banging on the door. Whatever he'd seen must've upset him greatly.

He whipped around and started running back. I could see on his face he had no idea where he was going, therefore, I would have to guide him back to the cell. After watching him struggle for a few seconds, I muttered: "This way!"

Further navigation with my help had him reach his cell, where he belonged. I must admit, it had been a close call but the adrenaline made it worthwhile. My new pet was certainly pleasing.

# Shattered Glass

 DECIDED to cool things down after our little adventure, so I ignored the boy for a week. His trial was due and that would be a trauma-tizing ordeal for him. I knocked on the pipe and wondered if he would answer. He did, and sounded petrified.

According to my report, he had been injected with a placebo but I thought I would torment him some more. Over the years, I witness many clinical trials go wrong so I asked about the negative symptoms most associated with the drug they were currently testing.

"Look at the colour of your fingers," I whispered urgently. "Do they seem darker? Black, even?"

That scared him, ha! He enquired about his sister again, which began to annoy me. I fed him more lies about discovering where she was kept. I even suggested I would let him out again to find her. Why not? He was harmless, really.

The next night, we continued our game in the dark. I unlocked his cell and started pacing back through the corridor. I smashed a light bulb on the way and headed further down. Then, I froze when I noticed him a mere couple of metres away from me. He must've moved faster than the last time—cocky bastard.

I demolished the next bulb but it was too late, he'd already seen me. I hoped he'd only glimpsed my shape and not the face. Acting quickly, I disappeared round the corner. I'm not entirely sure what the boy did next. I'd panicked when he spotted me and lost sight of him. That was nerve wracking.

I retreated back to the nurses' station where I contemplated how to proceed. The whole situation proved too risky. I felt stupid for letting him out of my sight. After ten minutes, I smashed the glass and pressed the fire alarm. The siren penetrated the deepest parts of my brain.

# TGN1412

O<small>F</small> course, there was no fire and I had to explain why I'd raised a false alarm. I lied my way out of the predicament, at the same time relieved the boy had made it back into the cell undetected, for my sake rather than his.

I got spooked after that. It really shook me up and realized I had to tone it down. I heard he had a panic attack shortly after and demanded to see his sister.

They dealt with his request promptly. The lad was knocked out and injected again. The more I thought about our conversations, the more I started feeling sorry for him. I felt such relief when he called my name and rescued me out of my reverie.

"Are you down there, Taisiya? I need to speak with you! Hello?"

I asked him how he was and how he felt after the injection. He seemed surprised, as if he'd forgotten all about it.

"I feel fine. It was just another placebo…" Demyan answered.

I knew different. That was why I agreed to help him escape when he asked me. The boy had been injected with the real drug, TGN1412, and according to our data, his chances of survival were miniscule. The other test subjects were not responding well to it. Demyan didn't have long to live and I had no doubt, he wouldn't get far. So I agreed to help, just to keep his hopes alive.

I supported his fantasy and played along with it. He tried to convince me to rescue his sister too, but that was out of the question. She had been transferred to another cell and watched closely for progress.

"I should be able to collect the supplies by tomorrow night…" I assured him. And I did.

# Blackened

 OPENED the cell for the last time and watched him swing the supplies over his shoulder. As the boy limped through the darkness towards the exit, I followed close behind. According to the test reports, the drug would be taking effect soon. I couldn't predict how his body would respond to it but if it was anything like the others, he would collapse in agony...

He approached the doors and I watched his every step with anticipation. Demyan pushed the bar open and started putting on the clothes I prepared for him. I was really anxious and thought for a moment he might actually escape but then, he removed the gloves and his expression changed to one of horror.

His fingers blackened and he collapsed soon after. I rushed to his side.

"Demyan! Wake up! Do you hear me? Demyan!" I screamed.

The boy mumbled something about dying and I tried my best to comfort him. When I whispered my name, he slipped into a coma.

# The Messenger

HE boy died shortly after his collapse. Most of his organs failed to function, so the doctors swiftly gave up on him. The drug was a disaster and I was sure they were going to scrap it after yet another incident. I felt it was my duty to inform his sister, however disturbing that might be.

I snatched my cell keys from the table and strolled down to the lower levels of the institution. I opened the door, entered with a solemn expression, and sat on the bed.

"Hello, how are you feeling, dear?" I asked.

We exchanged pleasantries and eventually approached the sensitive subject...the demise of her brother. As expected, the child was devastated. My attempts at comforting her proved futile and she kept crying and crying. It made me realise just how much she loved and depended on the boy. Akilina's world crumbled when her brother was no longer part of it.

As I watched her suffer, something changed in me. In my profession, I was expected to keep a professional distance and not get emotionally attached, but I couldn't help myself. Perhaps it was true that we get more sentimental as we grow older.

I left the girl alone for several weeks to give her time to mourn, and also to distance myself from her. I never cared for her brother much but I began to develop strange feelings for Akilina.

She was so pure and innocent. I didn't want her to share the same fate as her brother. So I decided—I would help her escape.

I would really help her escape.

# Ties That Bind

 N my next visit, we spoke about the boy for a long time. I confessed to Akilina about my deception, how I misled her brother and truly regretted it... Well, I never mentioned that for me, it had been just a game, at least at first—never told her how her brother had never roused pity or any sort of affection in me. It was imperative she trust me, for I needed her forgiveness and truly wanted to set her free. I'd changed...all because of Akilina...

It took some convincing but eventually, the child agreed to cooperate. We discussed the plan I formulated. She began to tremble so I hugged her, whispering soothing words into her ear. I assured her everything would work out just fine.

I had the provisions already packed and collected her soon after dinner. For obvious reasons, I chose an evening when I was the only nurse on duty and the institution was quiet. Still, it would be dark soon and the child had a long journey ahead of her. We had to hurry. It would be catastrophic if she got lost in the dark—she wouldn't stand a chance of surviving in the cold.

"Hurry, child, we don't have much time," I urged as I opened her cell.

She reached for her stupid book, ignoring the urgency in my voice. I put it in the backpack and grabbed her hand.

"Hurry, we must run!" I muttered.

We roamed the corridors for several minutes before finding the fire exit I selected for her escape. Throwing the backpack on the ground, I started dressing the child. She needed many layers, the more the better. It was extremely cold outside and she had a long walk to conquer.

"It's very cold outside. You need to wear all these layers," I said to her whilst pulling the sweater over her head.

When she was ready, I shoved the map in her small hand. It didn't occur to me that she was too young and might not be capable of reading maps. Luckily, the markings I made were really simple and she understood it.

I pushed her through the exit. "When you get to the hut, wait for me there and I will collect you soon," I promised her.

Then, I closed the doors and saw her no more.

# The Madam

HE minute I shut the door, the alarm went off. I panicked and quickly returned to the nurses' station. Two guards stood there, armed and waiting.

"Nurse Taisiya, come with us now. The Madam wants to see you," they said.

I swallowed, trying to be indifferent to my summoning.

The Madam had been in charge of the institution for as long as I could remember and ruled with an iron fist. She was a hard woman, bitter and cold—had never married although she had two children she did not care for.

An ultimate control freak, obsessed with power and not caring for anyone except herself... that's who the Madam was. I heard a rumour recently that she'd once condemned her own children to this place. I did not believe it. Despite her selfishness, surely even she wouldn't be capable of such cruelty?

My knees shook as I walked up the stairs to her office. The guards carefully watched my every move. Oh yes, I was in deep trouble. Only serious issues were handled by the Madam personally.

I knocked and entered her office after several seconds. She sat in her leather cathedra and immediately penetrated me with a contemptuous gaze.

"Nurse Taisiya, some distressing news has reached me about your personal involvement with certain patients of ours," she began.

I was not offered a drink, or a chair.

"Indeed, I hear that you conspired against me and helped one of them escape! What have you got to say for yourself?" she demanded.

Her hateful eyes made me uncomfortable as I tried as well as I could to conceal my guilt. "These accusations are false, Madam. I've worked here for over twenty years! If there was an escape, it had nothing to do with me," I concluded.

She smirked. "Don't play with me, Taisiya! You think your little conversations with my son went unnoticed? Everyone watches everyone in this place and they all work for me. I hear everything—your conversations, your little adventures in the corridors at night... and I know for certain YOU helped my daughter escape!" the Madam barked while pointing a finger in my face.

I went speechless and crippled with shock. Demyan and Akilina were her children?

She must've spotted the astonishment in my eyes.

"Ah, you're surprised. You're not going to get all judgemental on me, Taisiya, are you? Yes, I never loved my children. I didn't want a cripple and a retard for a son and daughter. Don't look at me like that! You've been here for over twenty years, for Christ's sake! You know what we do here and you never had a problem with it. Why now?" the Madam asked.

"But your own children... " was all I could say.

She shook her blonde head in disbelief. "Why am I even justifying myself to you? I summoned you here to inform you that my daughter won't get far. She was also injected with TGN1412 at her last trial and will probably suffer the same fate as my son, unless she has some miraculous reaction to the drug—which is very unlikely. All your efforts were for nothing and she's probably dead already. I'm deeply disappointed in you, Taisiya.

Believe me, your actions and ill judgement will have consequences. I am yet to decide what to do with you. Go home now."

"I'm sorry, Madam," I said but was dismissed with a wave of her hand. As I descended the stairs from her office, I couldn't stop smiling. The Madam forgot that, as a head nurse, I had access to all the scheduled trials.

On the night of Akilina's last trial, I swapped the injection containing TGN1412 with a placebo. She was probably inside the hut now, warming herself by the fire.

# Full Circle

PICKED up my things, ready to go home for the night. Akilina was no doubt anxiously waiting for me and I had to collect her soon. I wasn't sure if it would be safe or not for me to make a move. What if Madam's people were watching me?

I had to risk it anyway. The thought of Akilina being all by herself, terrified, in the abandoned hut, was more than I could take...

I left the institution and headed for the train station, which was located fifteen minutes away. At this late hour, the train was nearly empty. It took two stops to reach the point where I needed to get off.

I walked for another ten minutes through the Siberian snow, desperately searching for the hovel. The visibility was low and I worried I may not even find it in the dark.

More long minutes passed until at last, I spotted a small shape in the distance. As I got closer to the construction, I realised something was wrong. No light could be seen in the window. The hut sat in pitch black darkness. What was going on? Couldn't she get the fire started? Perhaps she didn't know how...

I approached the window and looked inside. The hut still appeared deserted. I leaned against the wooden door and pushed it open. When I ignited the oil lamp, the room was illuminated at once. Then, I gasped. The dwelling was empty, with no signs of human presence.

Where was she?

Printed in Great Britain
by Amazon.co.uk, Ltd.,
Marston Gate.